MARGRET & H.A.REY'S

Curious George's
Dream

Illustrated in the style of H. A. Rey by Vipah Interactive

Houghton Mifflin Company   Boston

The text of this book is set in Adobe Garamond.
The illustrations are watercolor and charcoal pencil, reproduced in full color.

Library of Congress Cataloging-in-Publication Data

Curious George's dream / based on the original character by Margret and H. A. Rey.
p.   cm.
Summary: A curious monkey who is tired of being small dreams of being big but discovers
problems with that as well.
RNF ISBN 0-395-91905-3 PAP ISBN 0-395-91911-8 PABRD ISBN 0-395-92342-5
[1. Monkeys—Fiction. 2. Dreams—Fiction. 3. Size perception—Fiction]
I. Rey, Margret, 1906–1996. II. Rey, H. A. (Hans Augusto), 1898–1977.
PZ7.C9225 1998
[E] —dc21   98-14163
                                                             CIP AC

Manufactured in China

This is George.

George was a good little monkey and always very curious.

After a long day at the amusement park with his friend, the man with the yellow hat, George was tired and glad to be home.

Soon dinner was ready. But when George sat down to eat, he was too small to reach his plate.

"I'm sorry, George," the man said. "I forgot to fix your chair."

He put a large book on George's chair and George climbed up.

As he sat on the book that was set on his chair, George thought
about his day. All day long he had been too small...

"Your hands are too little to hold these baby bunnies," the manager of the petting zoo told him.

"I'm sorry," said the man operating the carousel. "I cannot let you on. You need a grownup to ride with you."

MUST BE
THIS TALL

"Maybe next year," said the man taking tickets at the roller coaster.

7

But after a good meal and a good dessert, George began to feel better. When the dishes were finished, the man said, "George, I have a surprise for you," and they went into the living room.

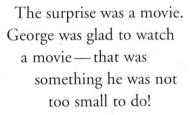

The surprise was a movie. George was glad to watch a movie—that was something he was not too small to do!

George was enjoying the movie, but it had been a full day and now he had a full stomach. Soon he could not keep his eyes open. The next thing George knew,

10

he was back at the petting zoo!
But this time something was
different: the petting zoo was
very small. In fact, everything
was small.

George looked around.
Then he looked at himself.
Maybe everything wasn't so
small after all, he thought.
Maybe he was . . .

BIG!

Uh-oh! This is not right, thought George. Then he remembered
the bunnies. Why, he was not too small to hold a bunny now. He was
not too small to do anything! What fun! George thought, and he went

to the bunny hutch. Now George could hold LOTS of bunnies, and he cuddled them to his face.

The bunnies liked George...

but the manager of the petting zoo did not.
"Put those bunnies down," she said. "You'll
scare them. You are too big!"

George didn't want to scare
the bunnies. He put them
down and turned to go.

Then George saw
the roller coaster.
He was curious.
Was he big enough
to ride it now?

Of course he
was big enough! If
only he could find a
seat big enough for him...

But the man taking tickets made George leave. "You cannot ride
this ride," he said. "You are too big!"

George was sad he could not ride, but he did as he was told.

"Catch that monkey!" someone yelled as George was leaving the roller coaster. "He's dangerous!"

People in the park became frightened. They began to run. They ran in all directions; but mostly, they ran AWAY from George.

George felt awful. He didn't want to frighten anyone.

PLEASE NO RUNNING

FERRIS WHEEL

ROUND UP

CAROUSEL

He just wanted to hide. But where could he go? He was too big to fit anywhere. Then George saw the carousel. He wouldn't need a grownup to get on with him this time.

But this time George wished he had a grownup with him...

he wished his friend were here.

George sat on the carousel feeling lonely. Suddenly, someone called his name. "George? George?" It sounded like the man with the yellow hat! Could his friend be here to take him home?

George heard his name again.

It was his friend!

George wanted to jump into his friend's arms, but the man with the yellow hat was too small. How could he ever take George home now? The man called his name again . . .

"George," he said. "Wake up. It's time for bed. You fell asleep watching the movie."

George looked at his friend.
Why, he wasn't small after all.
George looked at himself. He
was not big!
Now George could jump into
his friend's arms — and that is
what he did.

As the man with the yellow hat tucked him in, George was happy to be in his little bed. It was not very big, he thought. But he fit in it perfectly.

George was just the right size.